T0196263

Finding Balance

A Collection

Sharon L. Davis

AuthorHouse™
1663 Liberty Drive
Bloomington, IN 47403
www.authorhouse.com
Phone: 1-800-839-8640

Published by AuthorHouse 12/8/2011

ISBN: 978-1-4678-7048-1 (sc)
ISBN: 978-1-4678-7047-4 (e)

Printed in the United States of America

Any people depicted in stock imagery provided by Thinkstock are models,
and such images are being used for illustrative purposes only.
Certain stock imagery © Thinkstock.

This book is printed on acid-free paper.

On the seesaw of life….

To friends who've smoothed the plank…

To Matt and Megan, the angels lifting my shoulders…

To Leola, Lowell, Lowell W., and DeLane, the strengths
of my pivot….

To Mike, who sits behind me and watches my back…

To God, my counterweight…

Many thanks.

CHANCES

Madeline stared out the window of her Civic at the "Welcome to Willow Falls" sign. Confident she could accomplish her mission, she turned at the second signal light and finished her trip to Wallingford Manor.

As she drove through the familiar iron gates, Madeline thought of the last time she visited. Grams and Grandpa moved slower and had rested more. The five years she lived with them, they were vibrantly active. Until her last visit, Maddie thought they would live forever. She realized time touched even her grandparents.

Madeline pulled the Civic to a stop on the drive of the summer house. For forty years the Hudsons lived here. Before Madeline closed the car door, Grandpa walked from behind the house and Grams ran to squeeze her in a hug.

The tedious drive from Winston tired her. In the house, Madeline flopped on the daybed in her old room. Grams sat down beside her. Grandpa put her suitcases inside the door and went back outside to his work. Madeline rolled over on her stomach to face Grams and noticed the tight lines around her grandmother's mouth. Two days ago, Madeline had called. Grandpa seemed happy, yet his voice resonated with an unspoken concern. That unspoken concern bothered Madeline enough to prompt this visit.

Grams' fingers fumbled nervously with her handkerchief. This nervousness and the new tension wrinkles reinforced Madeline's premonitions that something was amiss.

"Tell me what's wrong, Grams. Is one of you ill, and you're not telling me?"

"Nothing's wrong, Maddie. Everything's fine."

Maddie sat up beside her grandmother. Taking one of her hands, Madeline scolded, "This is me you're talking to, Grams."

Reluctantly, Mrs. Hudson replied, "You know Mr. Wallingford passed away last month."

Madeline nodded. She read about Jonathan Wallingford III's death in the financial section of the newspaper. Madeline had liked Mr. Wallingford, a financial genius. He had been exceptionally kind to her grandparents and to her.

"Mr. Wallingford allowed us to live here even when we were old enough to retire. He and David played chess every Tuesday night."

"And?" prompted Madeline.

Tears shone at the corners of Grams' eyes. Mrs. Hudson looked down, trying to hide the tears from her granddaughter. "Oh, Maddie, we didn't want you to worry. It's young Mr. Wallingford, Jonathan. When Mr. Wallingford fell ill, Jonathan came home from their offices in Europe. Mr. Wallingford made Jonathan executor of his estate."

Madeline thought back to one summer vacation when the son lived in the manor. He was older than she, sat in the gardens reading books, and never spoke to her or to her grandparents.

"A lot of sons take over for their fathers, Grams. Tell me what's wrong with that."

With a sigh, Mrs. Hudson replied, "He's given us a month to vacate the summer house. He wants to hire someone younger to care for the manor." Looking at

Madeline, Grams sobbed, "Oh Maddie, what will we do? Where will we go? We've lived here for forty years! This is our home. We're too old to start over some place new. We have a small nest egg set aside, but without income, how will we ever manage?"

Madeline hugged her grandmother tightly. In her mind, Madeline sorted through her plans to move her grandparents to Winston. A wonderful village for seniors operated five miles from her condo complex. The arrangements she discussed with the village's administration before her trip could be finalized if her grandparents agreed. The Hudsons could move in within a month. Madeline related all of this to her worried grandmother.

Grams dried her eyes with her handkerchief. "Bless you, darling. I don't know what we would do without you. For more reasons than one."

"Don't you worry, Grams. You'll see. Everything will work out fine."

Mrs. Hudson patted Madeline on the cheek. "I'll go now and let you get unpacked."

As she unpacked her suitcases, Madeline got angrier and angrier. Jonathan Wallingford IV. How could he ignore her grandfather's forty years of faithful service to his family? Of course, this made her mission of convincing her grandparents to move to Winston a lot easier. Still, the Wallingford heir's thoughtlessness made her extremely angry.

Putting the last things away, Madeline decided to walk over the gardens surrounding the summer house. Taking care of the manor was the pride of her grandfather's life. Her parents died when she was fifteen, and Madeline lived at the manor until she left for college. She went away to private school during the school year, but she always helped Grandpa during the summers. She loved the gardens as much as her Grandpa did. Not a large estate, Wallingford

Manor could prove to be an overwhelming responsibility for an older man. Madeline needed to see for herself if Grandpa were still keeping the grounds in order.

Madeline stood facing the sprawling mansion, its beautiful but imposing exterior intimidating in the fading sunlight. Somewhere inside those walls walked the man who had broken her grandparent's hearts.

Madeline glanced around at the landscaping. Perfect. Now she was really upset! Squaring her shoulders, she looked again at the house. Back in Winston when Madeline squared her shoulders, her colleagues moved out of her way. Madeline meant business. Mind focused, she crossed the grounds to the manor's front door.

Lifting the brass knocker for the third time, Madeline impatiently tapped her size six shoe against the wooden porch. Except for the elder Mr. Wallingford and Jennings, the butler, Madeline had never met anyone from the manor house. Slowly the door opened. An older version of Jennings stood inside. Surprise! Wonder why Mr. Wallingford IV let Jennings stay? If her grandfather were too old to be a caretaker, Jennings was certainly too old to be a butler.

"Yes, miss?" Jennings looked down his nose at her.

"Hello, Jennings. I'm here to see Mr. Wallingford."

Jennings sniffed. "Mr. Wallingford is not receiving visitors this afternoon. Perhaps you could call for an appointment."

"I'm Madeline Murphy, Jennings," she reminded him, putting both fists on her hips. "Don't you remember me? I'm the Hudsons' granddaughter."

Jennings leaned forward and stared harder. Drawing back to his full height, he replied, "Yes, miss, I do remember you. However, Mr. Wallingford is still not receiving visitors."

"Whether he's receiving or not, I want to speak to him. Now."

Jennings saw the determined look in Madeline's face. Clearing his throat, he answered, "Very well, miss. Wait a moment. I'll speak to Mr. Jonathan." Moving aside so Madeline could enter the foyer, Jennings closed the door and disappeared down the hall.

Madeline inspected the foyer and its expensive furnishings. Her anger grew. There was so much in this manor. Her grandparents possessed so little. Now Wallingford wanted to take even that little away. Madeline seethed by the time Jennings returned.

"Mr. Jonathan will see you in the library, Miss Murphy. Fourth door on the left."

Madeline pushed open the library door. Late afternoon sun dappled the floor. The smell of leather and old pipe smoke filled her nostrils. The man behind the desk sat in shadows so that Madeline could not see his face. She didn't have to see his face to tell him what was on her mind. Angry words tumbled out.

"I'm Madeline Murphy, David Hudson's granddaughter. I want to know why, after forty years of faithful service to your father, you've decided to kick my grandparents out of their home. From the looks of the grounds, Grandpa's still able to do his job. How could you be so heartless? To kick him out of his home is one thing, but to make him feel useless and unwanted at his age – that's unconscionable!"

The man behind the desk rose. His handsomely bearded face and dark eyes became visible as he moved forward in the fading light. Madeline gulped as he walked from behind the desk to tower over her. With amused cynicism, he replied in a deep voice, "So I've damaged Mr. Hudson's pride, have I? Why didn't he tell me himself?"

"He's too much a gentleman. And you don't have a

clue about how Grandpa feels! To have little besides what you've worked hard to create and maintain, to take pride in what you do every day, and then to have everything taken away when you need it the most – what could someone like you, who's had everything handed to him, possibly know about how Grandpa's pride? Besides, complaining would embarrass him."

Anger darkened the man's face. "Who are you to say these things? You don't know me or the reasons for my actions. I've decided to let a good man go from a job that is too much for him to handle. I meant him no insult. I don't appreciate your insinuations, either. You don't know me well enough to pass judgment on the reasons for my actions."

His aloofness matched Jennings'. His words angered Madeline even more. "Have you looked at the grounds? They look like they've been manicured! You don't care at all whether Grandpa is capable of doing his job. You see him as too old and replaceable. This place has been his life for forty years! Do you know anything about feelings? Or about life for that matter? Boy, what I could teach you!"

"Oh? You could teach me, could you? What kind of things could you teach me, Miss Murphy?"

"Well, for instance, things like treating people with respect. There's more to dealing with people than looking at ages. Things like making people feel useful and appreciated. Thanking them. Grandpa is older, but he feels things deeply."

Madeline looked into Jonathan Wallingford's dark eyes. The anger in his eyes faded. A softness, a look of vulnerability appeared instead, followed by a sad loneliness. Her feminine instincts made her step closer to him. For some strange reason, Madeline placed her hand on his chest. Jonathan glanced down at her tiny hand then back at her face. Madeline blushed and quickly moved away.

"I'm sorry," she said, stepping back. "I really believe Grandpa should retire, too. I came to convince him and Grams to move closer to me. I just think you could have been kinder in letting him go. I won't waste any more of your time." Practically sprinting into the hall, she closed the door to the library.

Jennings was no where in sight. Madeline let herself out the front door. In the gathering twilight, she ran across the lawn to the summer house's welcoming lights. She walked to the patio and through the French doors into her room. Studying her reflection in the dresser mirror, she realized she had left Jonathan Wallingford with a confused look on his face.

During the next two days, Madeline helped her grandparents sort and fill boxes. That evening as Madeline soaked for an hour in a fragrant tub, she thought about her encounter with Jonathan Wallingford. What kind of a man was he? Apparently he was still unmarried. Was he lonely? Sometimes she felt lonely. She missed her parents. Grams and Grandpa loved her, but sometimes she longed for more. Did Jonathan Wallingford have anyone now that his father had died? Was he so thoughtless because he was all alone? He had everything money could buy, but money couldn't hug a lonely heart.

After her bath, Madeline snuggled down on the chaise beside the French doors in her room with a book. Her grandparents had been asleep for a long while. After a few minutes of reading, Madeline got an eerie feeling that she was not alone. Looking over the top of her book, she glanced out at the patio beyond the doors.

In the moonlight she saw Jonathan Wallingford. Startled, she sat upright, dropping her book. He mouthed, "Can we talk?"

Glancing at the clock by her bed, she mouthed back, "It's very late."

He nodded, "Just a few minutes?"

Madeline unlocked the door and stepped outside. The soft folds of her white sundress swirled about her body in the warm night breeze.

Jonathan motioned to a chair. "May I sit down?"

"Sure." Madeline sat down across from him. "My grandparents are sleeping. Please talk quietly. What did you want to say?"

Jonathan looked at her. In the light filtering through the doors, his face looked handsome, relaxed. In this light he didn't look like a monster. "We got off on the wrong foot the other day," he began. "I've been thinking a lot about what you said. I didn't intend to hurt your grandparents – or you – by doing what I thought was best. I've taken care of my father's business by computer and texts for so long, maybe I have lost touch with the human aspect of dealing with people. I came to apologize, first to you, and then to your grandfather. After living here all these years, I'm sure this place means more to him than it does even to me."

Madeline smiled. "I'm glad you changed your mind. I really want my grandparents to move closer to me, but I want the choice to be theirs, not a choice they're forced into making. Grandpa will appreciate you talking to him tomorrow."

Madeline attempted to stifle a yawn. Looking at his watch, Jonathan said, "I'm sorry, it's really late. Thanks for letting me apologize."

As he stood to leave, Madeline offered, "I apologize, too, for my behavior. I can be overly protective where my grandparents are concerned. Thanks for coming over."

When Jonathan reached the patio's edge, he turned. "I'll say goodnight, Miss Murphy, but only on one condition."

Madeline cocked her head. "Which is?"

"You told me the other day you could teach me things. 'Things about people and about life,' I believe you said. I'd like my first lesson tomorrow, please. Say, around lunch?"

She thought about his request. What could a few hours away from packing hurt? "Okay. How about a picnic?"

"A picnic? I haven't been on a picnic since... I don't remember my last picnic. Probably when I was a kid. Until noon tomorrow, Miss Murphy."

"Until tomorrow, Mr. Wallingford."

After Jonathan left, in the morning's wee hours, Madeline wrestled with her decision to encourage her grandparents to move closer to her. Madeline knew her grandparents would be happier at Wallingford Manor than in any retirement village no matter how many great activities occurred there. Her careful planning suddenly seemed very selfish. If Jonathan Wallingford allowed the Hudsons to stay on at the manor, she would move closer to them instead. If she took the promotion Mr. Cane had offered her this week, she could work from anywhere with a computer. Her grandparents' happiness meant much more to her than her life in the city.

The next day presented itself with sun, cooler air, and blue skies. As Madeline packed the picnic basket with lunch, her grandmother watched.

"So, you're going on a picnic with Mr. Wallingford?"

"Yes, Grams."

"Do you suppose you could talk to him? About your grandpa, I mean?"

"Grams, are you asking me to beg for Grandpa's job back?"

"Oh, no, honey. I just thought maybe you could get Mr. Wallingford to talk to David."

Madeline smiled, "Just teasing, Grams. Besides, I believe

Mr. Jonathan Wallingford has had a change of heart. I think he's already made up his mind to talk to Grandpa without any encouragement from me."

"What makes you say that, Maddie?"

"Trust me, Grams. Everything is going to be just fine."

Jonathan arrived at the summer house a quarter to twelve. Madeline's picnic basket was ready. So was a beautiful quilt Grams had pieced. She handed both to Jonathan. The two strolled over the grounds until Jonathan asked, "How about this spot, Miss Murphy?"

Madeline took in the green grass, the stone bridge, the hill's slope gently rolling down to a lazy stream. "Perfect."

After they had eaten, Madeline looked around at the green grass and the swaying trees. "You may not have been on a picnic in a while, but I must say, Mr. Wallingford, you certainly know how to pick the spot for one."

"Jonathan," he interjected. "Please call me Jonathan. Mr. Wallingford was my dad's name."

"Jonathan," she echoed, letting the word roll off her tongue.

Jonathan stretched out on the quilt and patted his full stomach. "If picnics are this good, I should have been going on them quite often." Turning his head and shading his eyes with his hand, he looked at Madeline. "If such good food is a part of my education, then I'm all for more learning!"

Madeline had a thought. Springing to her feet, she said, "Speaking of learning, time for lesson two!"

"What?" Jonathan asked lazily. As he watched, Madeline climbed the slope to the top. "What are you doing?"

"Lesson two is about having fun! Come on, Pokey, or I'll give you a bad mark for poor conduct!"

Reluctantly Jonathan left the quilt and climbed the hill to stand beside her.

"This is a game kids love to play. It's called 'Follow the Leader.' Just do what I do!"

Lying down parallel on the hill's top, arms and legs straight out, Madeline rolled down the slope. "Your turn!" she called from the bottom.

"Oh, brother," Jonathan grumbled. He looked down at his spotless tennis shorts. "I don't think I'm cut out for this."

"Don't be so stuffy! Are you going to let me teach you or not?"

"I suppose," he surrendered, shrugging his shoulders.

Lying down, he mimicked Madeline's actions of rolling down the hill. However, Jonathan's larger body picked up more speed than Madeline's smaller one. She had stopped well away from the stream at the bottom. His momentum carried him right into the middle of the water. Sputtering, he stood up, dripping. Menacingly, he walked toward Madeline.

She saw the twinkle of mischief in his eyes. "Oh, no, don't you dare!" Madeline protested, backing away, her hands up in defense.

"Oh, yes, teacher. Time for some lessons yourself!"

Picking her up, he dumped her gently, rear first, into the water.

Before Jonathan could walk out of the water, Madeline grabbed his ankle and sent him sprawling on his belly. Soon they were soaking wet, laughing and playing in the stream like children.

Late one evening, Madeline walked out of her bedroom doors onto the patio. A movement startled her. She relaxed as she recognized Jonathan's shape separating from the shadows.

"You scared me," she smiled. At the serious look on his face, her smile faded.

"Come sit with me for a few minutes, Maddie," he said, taking her hand and pulling her toward a bench under the trees some distance from the patio.

The picnic had been such fun. Jonathan talked to Grandpa that night and invited the Hudsons to stay in the summer house as long as they wanted. He told Grandpa a man could be hired to help with the physically demanding jobs. Thrilled, the Hudsons began unpacking their things early the next morning.

The days after the picnic had passed in wonderful succession. Jonathan told her about his career. Madeline told Jonathan about losing her parents. The pretense of being lifelong friends, the sharing of secrets big and small had enveloped Madeline like a soft cocoon. For the first time in a long time she felt a sense of belonging. A sense of belonging to someone.

The man sitting beside her now reminded Maddie of the first day she walked into the Wallingford library. The twinkle in Jonathan's eyes from the picnic was gone. No smile curved the corners of his mouth. His face once again looked like carved stone.

"Maddie, I'm not really good at talking about feelings. When I'm playing, I can say all sorts of things. But to be fair, I need to talk to you. Seriously." Jonathan paused.

"A long time ago, I loved someone very, very much. I was young. She hurt me badly because she didn't share my feelings. Now, I'm thirty-seven years old. I thought work was all I needed. I gave up on having a second chance to experience feelings for someone. I accepted I would always be alone. This acceptance was fine until a few days ago. You see, this fiery sprite dashed into my dark library late one afternoon and turned my orderly life upside down."

Madeline sat quietly. When he didn't speak again, she asked, "What are you trying to tell me, Jonathan?"

Sighing, Jonathan stood and raked his fingers through his hair. Turning to look at her, he answered, "I don't even know, Maddie! All I do know is that I feel more alive when I'm with you. I miss you when I'm not. I know we've only been around each other a few days, but something has happened to me. I don't know what it is, but it's scary and wonderful at the same time."

"Scary? Are you saying that you don't want to risk having feelings for me but you want to know if I can have feelings for you?"

"That sounds pretty cold and selfish, Maddie."

"Is it true?"

"Do you have to be both beautiful and smart?"

Silence fell between them. Madeline knew she'd only be here a few more days. Sure, she planned to move closer to Willow Falls as soon as arrangements could be made. She might occasionally run into Jonathan. Then again, if he never wanted to see her, he wouldn't have to. He had offices in Europe. Chances were high that she'd never see him again.

Playing emotional games was of no interest to her. Games were for children. This interlude started with games, but she wasn't a young naiveté. Emotions were sprouting inside her.

Madeline walked to where Jonathan stood. This time she put both palms on his chest. Looking up into his eyes, she said, "Life always has risks, Jonathan, especially when emotions are involved. If you want to see me sometimes, that will be fine with me. If you're afraid I might hurt you and you don't want to risk that, we can say goodbye right now and never see each other again."

The stone of his face crumbled into softness. "Oh, Maddie," he murmured as he folded her into his arms. "Maddie. I don't know." After a few moments, he let her go and walked away into the darkness. This time when they parted, Madeline wore the confused look.

Early the next morning, Madeline packed her suitcases. Contacts about subleasing her condo waited in Winston. Phone calls for finding a new place near Willow Falls needed to be made. Once she busied herself, the days would be too full to remember the bittersweet times at Wallingford. Or Jonathan.

The brunch Grams prepared for the last day of Madeline's visit lay on the kitchen table. The Hudsons invited Jonathan two days ago to the brunch to thank him for allowing them to stay on at Wallingford Manor and as a send off for Maddie. Grandpa and Jonathan took third helpings of the meal, but Madeline barely tasted the delicious food.

"I'll take care of the dishes, Grams," Madeline said, carrying her barely touched plate to the sink.

"I'll help, too," Jonathan added.

As the older people walked out of the kitchen, Madeline stacked dishes. Carrying the stack to the sink, Madeline trembled so that a cup fell off the top and crashed to the floor. The cup splintered into pieces. Picking one up, Madeline cut her hand.

"Here, let me see that," Jonathan demanded as blood dripped to the floor.

"It's nothing," she protested.

Wrapping a napkin around her hand, Jonathan smiled. "It's my turn, teacher. Lesson one, how to stop bleeding."

After a couple of minutes, Jonathan inspected the cut. "Better. The bleeding is slowing down."

"It's fine," Madeline said, pulling her hand away and walking out through the sliding doors.

"Hey, what's wrong?" Jonathan asked, following her outside. "You didn't eat. Are you mad about breaking the cup or at me?"

Turning to face him, Maddie sniffed, "Our little game is over, Jonathan. I'm going home to Winston today, remember?"

Jonathan wiped away a tear sliding down her cheek with his thumb. "What if I said I don't want to play games anymore?"

"You are you, and I am me. We're from different worlds. We look at life from very different perspectives. I'll go back to my life, and you'll go back to yours. Two weeks can't make that big a difference, no matter how wonderful the two weeks were. I heard what you said last night. Loud and clear."

"Are you sure you heard me correctly?" he asked, raising her chin to make her look into his eyes. "Remember, I'm not very good at relating to people in person. Sometimes what I say comes out wrong." He stopped for a moment and looked down at her. "What if I said after a lot of thinking last night, I finally figured out what's important to me? That those frightening relationship risks don't scare me so much if the risks are with you?"

"What did you say?"

"I said I'm not afraid anymore," he answered, pulling her into his arms. "And I'm sadly in need of a permanent life coach. Do you know anyone willing to take me on and teach me how to take advantage of a lot of second chances?"

Pulling his face down to hers, Madeline smiled up at him through her tears, "Do I, Mr. Wallingford? Do I ever!"

Accelerate

Summer flies into the past
As quickly as spring melts winter's snow.

Vibrant memories
Of a gentle love,
Like banked embers, burn slowly to the edge.

Golden ashes of summer love blow away
Into oblivion.

Bittersweet

You're gone.

But your presence
Lingers on.

Things at home
Remind me of you
And of how quickly you moved on.

They also remind me love memories
Stay too long.

CAPTURED

So different yet needing the same things,
You can't see you reflect the inside of me.
I see the softness and warmth inside you.

Put aside your tough façade,
The not- needing-anyone lie you tell yourself.
You want me here, but for what? Can you say?

I feel useless, alone, your wife but not your lover.
Please be the inside you for me today.

Cocoon

Deep inside me lies something sleeping,
Innocent, fragile, precious, wild,
Waiting to bloom within gentle keeping,
Beautiful, pure, a sleeping child.

Take me away from all my worries.
Take me to where the air blows free.
Teach me to live above the hurry,
Stir awake the sleeping me.

DIVINE NIGHT

Be still, night bird, and hear the song
Echoing down the corridor of silence.
The soft bell of love rings
And breaks the night.

Oh, broken night, I'll remember you
When time's immortal globe lies shattered.
For love invaded my senses
In your silver silence.

DREAM CHILD

A gentle murmur in my heart
Floated upward to my mind
Then plummeted to find
A quiet place inside me.

A dream, a hope, a miracle
Became a tiny light
That chased away the night
From its place inside me.

Into the world from my heart
A gift, you became a hope
To help my tattered mind to cope
With the pain inside me.

Never, ever, could I have known
What sweet peace and joy you'd bring,
How great a gift would be this thing,
This love inside me.

ESCAPE

Look through my eyes, and we will share
All the secrets hidden there.
Live with my soul, and you will be
Everything you've ever dreamed.

Love with my love, and together we'll know
Everything we dream is so.
The magic guiding us will become
The true love sought by everyone.

ETERNAL CONSCIOUSNESS

Life goes on because of love,
Other things disappear.
Verses are written all in vain.
A word can't bring you near.

Yet on love's wings your presence
Comes floating to my mind
To nestle in my memory
And stay there for all time.

Closure

"Shut your eyes. In your mind go back to a time when you were ten. Remember how you felt. When you open your eyes, you won't see me, you'll see your father. Tell me everything you always wanted to say to me but never felt you could."

When she opened her eyes, Nett didn't see Dr. Bradley. She saw her father's face. Emotions smothered for eighteen years broiled. Words poured out, an emotional explosion.

"How could you? How could you treat a little boy that way? The day you brought home the tiny lawn chair, and I said, 'Look, Papa brought you a chair!' and you looked at me and said, 'I didn't bring it to him, I brought it to you.' He was only three, but I know he knew you left him out! How could you put me in that position? Did you not know it would break my heart, too?"

"You never told either of us that you were proud of us. But you were very quick to tell us when we did something wrong! You were so quick to discipline us. But how often did you just offer to hug us? We were so young, just little kids, but we knew we never made you happy, never measured up to some standard you had created. If you thought pride was a sin, you could have at least let us know you loved us just because we tried to make you proud."

"And the way you always yelled at Mom in front of other people! Didn't you care that you embarrassed her and made her feel awful? None of us could ever please you! It was like you were perfect and we never could be. No matter how hard we tried or didn't try."

"I hated you, hated you! And I loved you! That drove me to try to please you and stressed me so badly that I always made mistakes. Could you not see what you were doing to us? How emotionally messed up you were making us?"

As Nett made a left off the bridge, the memories of the day she had finally faced how she felt about her father flooded her mind. Driving home always made these memories resurface. Could she ever put these emotions to rest?

On that day of the explosion, for fifteen full minutes in Dr. Bradley's office, stuffed emotions had spewed from Nett. The torrent of hate and love raced from behind the façade of pretense and hope she had worked to build for years. Words she didn't know were in her head and feelings she had denied existed rose up like thorny arrows and shot out of her mouth.

When the words stopped, heaving sobs started. Her control over self had completely dissolved. The world in her mind collapsed, falling inward to smother her. The reality of her life stared her in the face. Nett felt very small and very vulnerable.

Eventually the storm of emotion had subsided. Through the blur of her tears, Dr. Bradley's face had slowly come into focus. Handing her a box of tissues, he smiled.

"I really thought we would have to put you in the hospital. I didn't think I could help you. You are the most emotionally shut-down person I've ever treated. I knew if I could make you feel something, we would have a chance. I'm sorry that anger is the easiest emotion to tap into. How are you feeling right now?"

Emotionally and physically exhausted, she had not wanted to talk. She had wanted to sleep.

"I'm very tired. May I go now?"

"Do you have someone to drive you home?"

Her mind settled on the man in the waiting room. The man so like her father.

"Yes."

"I think I need to see you a few more times. This week, try to be more honest with your emotions. Let people know when you are unhappy. It's not a sin to tell people when they offend or hurt you."

Driving to her parents' home on this late summer day, Nett recalled every detail of that day's events clearly. It was the first time she had allowed herself to admit she hated her father. And that she hated Allen for being like her father. Had it really been fifteen years ago? She flipped the turn signal and made a left turn. Memories came, too, about Allen.

Four years her senior, Allen married Nett after she attended two years of college. From the beginning, their relationship mirrored the problems of her relationship with her father. After seven long years of marriage, Nett stopped eating and talking. She couldn't remember her first sessions with the therapist. Dr. Bradley told Nett that she was like a placid lake on the surface. But under the smooth surface were old tires, stumps, garbage. She never found the courage to follow his advice to drain the surface and sift through the garbage. Then after the anger explosion, she finally tried to do what Dr. Bradley advised her to do. Nett spoke honestly about her feelings and needs to the people in her life.

Allen hated her when she told him things that bothered her. Self-focused, he blamed her for everything. Nett eventually grew strong enough not to allow Allen to emotionally assault her. Allen couldn't accept this new Nett.

He much preferred the acquiescent one. So, after nine years of marriage, they separated. Eventually, Allen divorced her on grounds of irreconcilable differences.

The relationship scars made some aspects of life and love impossible for Nett to handle. She didn't relate well romantically to men. In the years since her divorce, Nett ignored dating. After all, for nine years she had been a pro at ignoring things.

Turning onto the county road to drive the last twenty miles to her parents' house, Nett mulled over memories of the past five years. She heard Allen had married again. He had married a wonderful girl Nett knew in college. Nett heard they now had a little son and were living in Memphis, happy and contented. She could finally be glad Allen found happiness. Maybe she was even a little envious.

Over the past five years she had also tried to build a better relationship with her father. He still never said he was proud of her and never congratulated her on any of the awards she received at work. They had, however, finally become friends. They both loved junk and traveled at least two weekends a month to scour collections at local and distant flea markets. Nett found her father and she really loved to talk. She spent hours with her father in deep discussions over politics and Scriptures and people. In her heart, she forgave him for the things that had crippled her emotionally as a child. She realized his upbringing after the Great Depression in a poor sharecropper's family had originally crippled him and funneled his thinking into the father he had become. Papa had done his best in rearing her. He had not maliciously intended to skew her emotional balance.

Then the day last spring came when she looked up from her desk to see her sister standing at the door, her eyes full of tears. "The doctor told Dad to get his house in order," Laura sobbed, "He has from three to six months. It's pancreatic cancer." At that moment, Nett's mind raced. She couldn't breathe. This couldn't be! The family's doctor sent her father to the specialist for gall stones. Cancer! Her sister's tears drove the finality of the doctor's diagnosis home. Life without Papa? Five years ago this news would have bounced off the wall around her emotions. Now the word cancer crawled into the middle of her emotions where it exploded into a million painful shards.

Driving up the final quarter mile driveway to her parents' house, Nett felt as if she were moving in a dream. She had visited as often as she could during the six months of her father's illness. Her sister devoted herself to taking care of their dad during his last weeks. Laura slept in the floor of his bedroom so she could attend to his pain medication and physical needs. Nett couldn't bear to see him so frail and helpless. He had always been so strong, so indestructible. Memories of his last few weeks blurred into fuzzy pictures of bedside vigil, hospice nurse visits, morphine patches, and mouth swabs. Hours of watching the man she had most feared and most loved in her life waste away.

Nett pulled to a stop in front of her parents' house. Memories of the cold day when they scattered Papa's ashes in his favorite wooded spot came to her mind. Holding hands with all the family and saying a prayer. Numbness from the pain of witnessing his suffering days bled over into the grief of spending the rest of her life without him. He had been both a rock that crushed her and a rock she held on to for stability.

Nett went inside the house and hugged her mom. Thin from a fear of high cholesterol and from depressed loneliness, her mom kissed Nett's cheek.

"How are you, Mommie?"

"I'm okay. I'm taking care of myself, I promise you."

"You look like you've lost more weight."

"I haven't. I need to stay light to keep my knee from hurting."

Bluegrass gospel whispered from the radio in the living room. Papa's station. "Are the violets blooming yet?"

"Yes, they've been blooming for about a month."

"I think I'll walk down to the woods for a while. Do you want to come with me?"

"If it's okay, I think I'll just stay here. I'm a little tired today."

Nett kissed her mom's cheek. "I'll be back in a few minutes."

Nett walked out the back steps. Sun poured down on her head and shoulders. A year had passed. Short-sleeve weather finally, she thought. Memories of her little brother, a sled, and a hill covered with slippery pine needles drifted through her mind. Napping in the bed of Papa's pickup in the first sun of summer when she was a teenager. The time Papa tickled her nose with a fuzzy weed while she tanned. She swatted the weed, thinking it was a fly, until Papa giggled. Some memories were happy, normal.

Nett stopped by the marker at the edge of the place where Papa's ashes were strewn. Wild violets, her favorite flower, bloomed everywhere. They usually only lasted a week or two – Mommie said these had bloomed for at least a month. Realizing the extended length of blooming, Nett remembered a conversation she had with Papa about the violets last spring. Was it too much to think that God had let these purple faces last longer to cheer her up?

Walking on the path Papa had cut along the power lines for the dogs to run, Nett stopped. In her mind she so wanted to talk to her father one more time. There were so many memories, so many things she never got to say.

Aloud Nett said, "I miss you so much, Papa. I know we

didn't always get along, but for the past few years, you've been my best friend."

As tears rose in her eyes, she felt a bug land on her arm. She brushed her arm with her fingers. When she looked, there was no bug.

Looking around, she noticed the rest of the early blooming spring flowers. "No wonder you wanted us to put your ashes here. Look how beautiful all of these flowers are."

Again, the feeling of a bug landing on her arm. Again, no bug.

Next to her arm tall weeds with little fuzzy ends grew. But the wind wasn't blowing, and she had not moved. Smiling, she said aloud, "Is that you, Papa, playing with me?"

As the question left her lips, a sweet, floral smell wafted into her nostrils. Nett closed her eyes and breathed in the fragrance. When she opened her eyes, Nett walked to every bloom around her trying to find the ones she had smelled.

None of the flowers gave her the smell.

Then another memory passed through her mind. She heard sometimes when spirits say goodbye, the living people smell a sweet fragrance. As if the earth and everything on it held their collective breath, Nett froze.

"Was that you, Papa? Were you telling me goodbye?" she whispered, her eyes filling with tears. "Please forgive me for not always forgiving you. I know you loved me, even when you didn't show it. I understand now. I love you bunches."

As she said the words aloud, Nett's heart flooded with a peace and a joy that she had never experienced. In that moment, she gave forgiveness and felt forgiveness. Genuine love like a shower enveloped her from head to toe.

Nett knew in her heart wherever he was, her Papa was alright. For the first time in her life, Nett also knew that from now on, she would be alright, too.

LOVE'S PAIN

The pillow lies warm and hollowed
The imprint of your head.
I kissed the place where your lips had brushed
And wished for love and rain.

Come quickly, and tell me tales
Of things I've never seen or heard,
Fill up my senses with your words of love
And take away the pain.

Old Soul

You stood –
Always a little to the side,
Asking why
Other kids never laughed at your jokes
Like older folks.
I held you –
Protecting you tightly in my arms
From harm,
Praying that your golden insight
Would survive youth's nights.
You stand –
Almost a man.
You can face them all,
Your inner self secure.
You will endure.
I smile –
God blessed the world with you.
I always knew
That your gifts would help you become a man
Who would stand.
You stand –
Still a little to the side,
Now knowing why
You're here and who you'll become.
My dearest son.

On Stage

Raindrops slowly beat a rhythm
Against my window pane.
All my emotions crash with them.
I'll never touch you again.

Touching you for me meant a lifetime
For you, an act in life's show.
The only thing left me now is time.
How can I live? Why did you go?

Forever and a day will I love you.
Life's difficult now you're gone.
Dreary days demand payment due,
Love's game is over and you've won.

Touching you for me meant a lifetime,
For you, an act in life's show.
The only thing left me now is time.
How can I live? I miss you so.

Opaque Transience

If my heart could speak directly to yours,
If we could communicate without the hindrance of words,
Then love could grow.

If I could know you hear my heart,
If your listening were as clear as mine.
There would be no need for words.

But we cannot communicate without our words.
My lips stammer over the thoughts in my heart.
I don't know if you can understand.

Our possibility must fade into nothingness.
We must travel individual paths –
Separated by words.

PROMISES

Down a tree lined path,
I thrilled to a nightingale's song.
Thoughts tumbled, a color waterfall,
Broken scenes in my mind.

The moon shone, a pale disk in the sky,
Like the huge, ever watching eye
Of God.
Whispering through the trees
The fluttering of angel wings,
Songs of birds in the night,
Sounds beckoning to love and dawn.

A strong hand grasped my fingers
And a warm eye
Held my heart.
Oh, wildly beating heart!
In sync with tumbling thoughts
Beyond the night's quiet bendings.

Blessed moments spent in tenderness,
Night of nights, whose splendors shine
Weaving together the flutterings of time,
And the promises of enduring love.

RESEMBLANCE

His hair is burnished gold –
Gold found in the home of the dawn,
Gold spun from angels' harps –
Lying softly against my shoulder.

His lips bloom like red roses –
Red wine dripping from a glass,
Red blood beating softly in a heart –
Caressing my neck with kisses.

His voice flows like a gentle brook –
Soft breezes flowing through tall grass,
Downy feathers floating in sunlight –
Brushing my ear with his desire.

Rainbow joy he awakens in me –
Golden days promising safety,
Pale blue whisperings of silver lined days –
Mirroring my love in his laughing eyes.

SERENDIPITY

Love for me was a delicate whisper,
An illusive beauty, like sweet, fading dreams.

Then in your eyes, I saw love's reflection,
The secret of how dreamers fly without wings.

Soul Talk

I know you love me by the little things.

A quiet kiss when no one's looking,
The gentle pressure when you squeeze my hand,
Tenderness you show me in many ways.

I know you love me by the tiny whisperings
My soul hears from yours.

ESCAPE

An unearthly howl split the hellish air. Agony gripped every fiber of her body. The physical pain caused her to drift between lunacy and sanity. Time hung suspended in the pain and solitude.

The baby finally entered the world. Tiny, perfect, he mewed. Listening to him, she could only lie still, as still as death, unable to reach to take him in her arms.

In the recurring nightmare of her son's birth, this time the baby's crying changed. The sound deepened, expanded as it grew louder. Slicing into the space between sleep and waking, the thundering sound catapulted her into full consciousness.

Wide awake and frightened, she looked out across the parched landscape. Dust clouds swirled in the early morning light. Far to the north on the distant road, machines appeared, fading in and out of the dust like phantoms. Raucous yells and the engines' thunder flooded the lifeless air. Riders! Fear raced up and down her nerves, signaling her body to move.

Quickly, she reached into the crib and picked up the sleeping baby. Running down the back hallway from the kitchen, up the first flight of narrow stairs, past the landing, her bare feet flew up even more narrow stairs to the attic.

Behind the false wall in the tiny corner of the attic's darkness, safety waited for her and the baby.

She had discovered the hidden room in the old farmhouse's attic the week she and Kal moved in. Marrying Kal had given her a feeling of security and someone to love. Moving into the house with its three levels and bright rooms, the old farmhouse had added to those feelings. She had lived such an orphaned life until then. Exploring every inch of the house before the time for planting, she knew every plaster crack and creaking board within its four walls. Her back ached when she thought of all the work she and Kal had done to make the house livable and the fields fruitful. Kal bought an old tractor to help with the big fields, but she tilled the small kitchen garden with her own hands. She had cleaned and painted the house, tended the animals, canned the vegetables.

Then came the drought. Crops withered. Eventually the leaves on the big trees surrounding the house curled into tight spindles. After eight months, the drought caused all the neighbors to move to the cities for relief. Kal left, too, to find work, money, food, anything to help. Her food supply dwindled, the generator fuel ran out, the animals died. Now the farm's best promises lay as dry and brittle as the crops in the fields.

The attic blasted her with its stifling heat. Protectively clutching her tiny son, she pushed the door shut behind her. She pressed the button to open the hidden panel. She pushed the eaves' vent open to make sure air came in. She'd always stashed something away for emergencies. Her life at the shelters prompted that behavior. Seeing stashed provisions on the floor made her smile. Self preservation paranoia could be beneficial at times. Sliding down into the dust farthest from the panel, she waited.

Maybe the riders would not see the farm house. It did

sit quite a distance off the road. The clouds of dust stirred up by the bikes and cars would make visibility poor. The baby stirred. A discontented grunting and squirming accompanied his waking. Wetness rose on his downy head. Drops of sweat trickled down to pool at the small of her back. She quickly let the baby nurse to quiet him. She flicked a dry tongue over drier lips.

The thunder of the riders grew closer and closer until the engines roared to a stop in the yard below. Ugly, terrifying laughter and swearing floated through the vent. A door crashed off its hinges. Glass broke. Loud thuds shook the house as heavy furniture overturned. Muffled footsteps from thickly soled boots beat tympanic rhythms. Cabinet doors slammed open and shut.

After an eternity of yells and crashes, footsteps pounded up the main staircase. Crashes and shattering started anew. Loud curses bounced around the rooms.

Swearing and footsteps finally descended the stairs. In her arms, the baby purred himself back to sleep. All her muscles stretched taut as rubber bands. As the noises below faded, she slumped against the rough, attic wall.

A floor board in the attic creaked! She sat bolt upright. Eyes wide, nerves tingling, muscles twitching. She looked down at the baby. He slept quietly. Don't make any noise, don't even breathe, she thought.

In an instant the panel to her safe room slid open. Bright light from the attic windows momentarily blinded her. Large fingers curled around the panel. A huge, black figure blocked the window's light. Her eyes focused slowly – up the fingers to a muscled arm, a broad, leather-clad shoulder. There was enough strength in that arm to frighten her into total immobility.

Pale, piercing eyes captured hers. Nothing within her

remained secret under that stare. Helpless, she beheld this half-man, half-behemoth. Fear flooded her.

Stirring, the baby snuggled into the curve of her arm. His soft defenselessness stirred her mother's instinct. Surprised, she felt a growl rise from her throat, a warning.

While their eyes held – dangerous man, daring mother – a silent message passed between them. A mutually respected boundary seemed to keep both motionless. The man raised a gloved finger to his lips. Then he quietly closed the panel.

She listened to his footsteps on the narrow attic stairs. She heard the engines roar to life below. Her heart's pounding slowed with the fading thunder of the riders.

She waited until the baby waked to leave the attic. Clothes clung to her sweat-drenched body. Shakily she rose, her arms and legs tingling from prolonged disuse. She brushed the baby's damp, downy head with her lips. Salt. Cautiously, she descended the narrow attic stairs.

On the second floor, clothes and broken objects littered the rooms. Precious things carefully chosen with squirreled money lay in pieces. A final insult, the relentless dust sifted in to cover everything.

After Kal's long absence, she had cried and ranted and cried some more. How could he leave her, knowing she was pregnant? Part of her knew he thought she was safer, he would be back soon, he would be there when the baby came. Kal loved her, protected her. But days stretched into weeks without him. She knew something was wrong. If Kal were able, he would have come back to her. The radio reported lawless raiders who had banded together in the drought. Before he left, Kal cautioned her about hiding if strangers appeared. She wondered if he had heeded his own advice.

Alone for months, she decided she would cry no more tears. For any reason. Bewildered by the destruction the riders left behind, she choked back hot tears that gathered behind her eyes. Uncontrollable heaves started in her lungs and shook her body. She gulped for air, trying not to let the waves of sadness drown her.

Her heaving jostled the baby. He opened his eyes, the piercing blue that mimicked Kal's, and cooed softly. She felt a warm wetness against her belly. The heaves slowly subsided. Looking down at the tiny blessing in her arms, she moved to the bedroom for a diaper.

Upon inspection of the kitchen, she found it fared no better than the rest of the house. Little food remained. Dishes swept out of cabinets by angry arms lay in shards on the counter. Like the front door, the back door swung from the bottom hinge, the top one separated. Shaking her head, she stepped out into the rising heat of the day.

A hot wind blew across the empty yard. No cooling comfort came, though the wind stirred. Trickling down her neck, salty drops ran under her thin shirt. Between her breasts and shoulder blades, droplets chased each other to her waist. Like the wind's dryness, her perspiration failed to bring any coolness to her skin.

Past the midday point in the sky, the sun burned, pouring intense wrath on the tormented farm. Dry, brown grass curled against the soil's pale ash. The trees stretched dry branches upward, pleading to the merciless sky.

Spreading a quilt beneath a tree's dead shade, she laid the baby down. Out had to be cooler than in. The grass crackled under her knees as she placed the baby on the quilt. Contentedly he pounded the air and looked at her. Intense emotion grabbed her heart as she gazed into his perfect face. How long could she keep them alive on her own?

Wiping a trickle from her forehead, she glanced around. Nothing stirred in the barren yard, except for tiny dust devils rising in the tracks left by the riders. Water. She needed a drink.

The farm's water came from a deep well. With the generator, pumps filled the livestock pools and the house with cool, clean water. Thank goodness Kal built the windmill last year in case the generator's fuel ran out. She heard its blades clicking in the dry wind and licked her dry lips. Thoughts of a drink sent her into the kitchen. Discovering a small, unbroken jar, she headed to the windmill.

Under the tree, the baby contentedly paddled the air. Balancing him in one arm and the jar in the other, she started for water. The baby turned his head toward her, rooting for his own drink.

"My, but you're greedy, little one!" she smiled. "Always wanting to eat." Kissing him and holding him closer, she said, "Come with mama to get water. If I don't drink, neither will you."

Dust swirls rose behind her bare feet on the powdery path. Reaching the well, she used the hand pump to prime the water. She held the jar under the precious flow. She gulped the water. The baby blinked as some drops escaped down her chin to splinter on his tiny face. She smiled down at him. Refilling the jar, she balanced her precious loads and walked back to the house.

She laid the baby back on the quilt. Dampness on her shirt made her sigh, "You keep this up, and we'll have to let you go bare-bottomed," she smiled down at him as she went into the kitchen to look for a towel.

As she stepped back into the yard, she felt danger. A quick glance to the quilt showed the baby kicking merrily. But something made the hair on her neck prickle. Slowly, deliberately, she moved toward the baby. The morning's events unnerved her. Picking up her son, she spoke softly to him. She felt someone watching her. Quickly she glanced around the yard but saw no one. She started slowly toward the house.

Under one of the trees, a shadow moved. Detaching itself from the trunk, the shadow became a man. A huge man. A leather-clad, muscled, behemoth of a man. With piercing eyes.

Her breath caught in her throat. He watched her intently. Against the tree, his outline diffused to look even bigger. Fear froze her where she stood. The house would offer no shelter. The doors hung limply on their hinges. There was no where to run.

The man moved toward her a few steps. Muscles rippled on his thighs. Had she somewhere to run, he would outrun her easily. Like a mother bird billowing its wings to look bigger, she straightened to her full height and clutched the child protectively to her shoulder.

The man respected the remaining distance between them. His voice moved to her across the dry air, deep and melodic. "Don't be afraid. I didn't come back to hurt you or the baby."

"Why did you come back?" she tried to control fear's vibrato in her voice.

His pale eyes held hers captive. Quietly he said, "I'm not sure."

Remembering what his traveling companions had done to the farm house, she hissed, "Well, if it's to steal something, you've wasted time. Nothing here's worth anything now. Not even to me."

"I didn't come to take anything," he said, moving a few steps closer.

She backed away. "I don't know why you came back, but I want you to leave."

Gentleness in his bearded face unnerved her. His muscled power and the softness in his eyes confused her. Shrugging his massive shoulders, he said, "When we broke camp two days ago, I'd no place to go, except with the riders." He paused reflectively, "I've seen so much in the past year. Things that made me sick and ashamed." He paused. "I saw you today, so small and alone, holding your baby, with courage in your eyes. You reminded me of things I'd lost." He wiped his forehead with a handkerchief. "I'd forgotten anything good existed. Something in your eyes made me want to come back. To see if I could help you."

Shaking dark curls over a defiant shoulder, she blustered, "I can take care of myself."

His next question destroyed her bravado. "Where's your husband?"

Looking at her son's fist tangled in her hair, she replied, "I don't know."

Admitting the truth aloud broke through the hard line of defense she tried to maintain. Tears stung her eyes.

"How long has he been gone?" the man asked.

"I don't know," she murmured. "Months. Since before the baby was born. Seems like a lifetime ago."

All the emotions she fought so valiantly that morning overwhelmed her. Her legs gave way, and she buckled to the ground. Hot tears of anger, love, hurt, and fear rained from her eyes.

When the storm of emotions passed, she remembered she was not alone. She looked up. The man was gone.

Was she hallucinating? Dehydration caused hallucinations. Had she heard him speak? Had her loneliness dreamed him back just so she could talk to someone? So she wouldn't feel alone?

A crunching noise to the side of the house caused her to look. Drying the tears from her cheeks with the back of one hand, she saw the bike roll around the house. The man pushed it under the tree where he had stood and kicked it into an upright position. He opened two pouches slung across the back seat.

"If you'll let me come closer," he said. "I have food."

Food! Trying not to appear too eager, she nodded.

He moved across the yard to the quilt where she knelt. Grass crackled beneath his black boots. Squatting down, he carefully opened the bags and motioned for her to help herself.

Bread, cheese, jerky! Miraculously, saliva filled her mouth. Gently, she moved the baby to the curve of her arm. Sleepy and hungry again, he fussed, waving his tiny arms in protest. She could smell the food, its aroma insistent in her nostrils. She murmured soothingly to the baby.

The bearded stranger reached out huge hands toward the infant. Her mother's instinct moved the baby away from the man's hands. He smiled, his pale eyes staring guilelessly into hers.

"I won't eat him, I promise," he teased. "I used to be good with babies, a long, long time ago." An old pain flickered across his strong, brown face. "Let me entertain him while you eat."

His rough hands gently touched the baby. "What's your problem, little fella?" he asked, his melodic voice deep and soft. When his hand touched the back of the baby's diaper, he laughed. "I'd fuss, too, if I needed dry pants."

"I was just about to change him," she said.

"I can do it," the man laughed, picking up the dry towel from the quilt. She watched as her son grabbed handfuls of the man's beard. The man's huge hands adeptly changed the small boy's diaper. She smiled and reached for some food.

"Don't eat too fast," the man cautioned as she ravenously attacked the food. "You could make yourself sick. How long since you've eaten?"

"Real food?" she asked, her cheeks full. "I don't really remember." She made a concerted effort to slow her chewing.

Finishing, she glanced gratefully at the man. He smiled back, a clean smile, no shadows of expectations in his eyes. She relaxed a little more, her full stomach helping her to begin to trust him.

When the man smiled at her, the baby fussed, his tiny fists pummeling the man's bearded face. "I can see you're a fighter, little man!" he chuckled.

Her smile faded. "He's had to be."

The man looked up at her. Was that a look of admiration? She added, "But right now, I think he's just hungry."

"Well, I don't think I can help him there," the man smiled. His rough fingers slightly brushed against her arm as he handed her the baby. She blushed and looked away.

Looking toward the broken door, the man said, "I need to fix that before dark. Maybe it'll keep some animals out."

She started to tell him Kal said all the wild animals were either dead or gone, but she realized he might mean a different kind of animal. She watched as he moved toward his bike to retrieve a small bag of tools.

She turned away and let the baby nurse. She could hear the sounds of the door being fixed. The baby softly hummed himself to sleep. She laid him gently on the quilt. On her face the sunlight turned crimson as it headed toward the horizon.

She turned from the baby to watch the man work. He had taken off his leather vest and his shirt in the heat. The muscles along his shoulders and arms glistened with sweat in the red light. Things she had not thought about in months flashed through her mind. Hurriedly, she looked away toward the windmill.

The man finished and stepped back to survey his work. "Buskirk can be so destructive when the mood strikes him," he said, as he sat down on the quilt next to her and the sleeping baby.

"Buskirk?" she asked.

"The riders' leader," he answered.

Silence fell softly in the air between them, as the sun fell below the horizon. The sky glowed with twilight's pinks and purples. Stars peeked out of the deepening darkness.

"It's beautiful, isn't it?" she mused. "At sunset I can almost forget how bad things really are."

The man didn't answer. He studied her face with his pale, piercing eyes. She looked away. "You didn't tell me your name," she said, attempting to break the sunset's spell.

"Jeremiah," he replied. "Jeremiah Hawk. Most people call me Hawk." The name fit him well, fit the piercing watchfulness in his pale eyes. "What's yours?"

"Tela," she replied. Her fingers fidgeted nervously in her lap as the darkness deepened.

"Tela," he whispered drowsily, yawning as he lay down on the quilt beside the sleeping baby. "You're very beautiful, Tela," he said as he closed his eyes.

In moments, his breathing deepened to that of a sleeper. Tela smiled at his gentle snore. Her fears for the night faded. Picking up her son, she walked into the house through the repaired door and went to bed.

Tela stretched out on the bed. A tension between her shoulders that plagued her since Kal left slowly relaxed. Amazingly, she did not fear the stranger asleep under the tree. Something about his presence actually calmed her. A peaceful sleep washed over her tired mind, a restful sleep. She was no longer alone.

Tela awoke to food smells. Lazily she sniffed the tantalizing odor wafting through open windows. In his crib, the baby still slept peacefully. Tela wondered if he, too, somehow felt safer since Hawk's arrival.

Padding quietly down the hall to the kitchen on bare feet, Tela raked fingers through her dark curls. How wonderful it would feel to have a shower. She had saved water, afraid to use it for more than sponging off and washing her hair. To be wet from head-to-toe with water instead of perspiration!

The tempting odor of food pulled Tela through the house and outside. In the yard Hawk watched something cooking on a spit over a small, carefully tended fire. He did not notice her arrival. She could count the muscles on his bare back and along his arms as he banked the coals to prevent any sparks from going astray.

Tela cleared her throat. Hawk turned quickly. His face relaxed when he saw her. "Good morning," he smiled.

"For once, Mr. Hawk, I believe it is a good morning," she replied.

Hawk flipped the spit to cook the other side, "Hungry?"

"Always. I think I could eat for a hundred years and never be full."

After silent moments, Hawk murmured, "If you'll let me, I'll take care of you and the baby. You'll never be hungry again." His pale eyes pierced into hers. In them she saw something that caused nervousness and exhilaration to swirl upwards inside her at the same time.

The baby cried. Tela turned and walked back into the house.

While the baby nursed, Tela sat on the bed and thought about Kal. He'd been gone such a long time. Should she continue to wait here for him? Was he still alive? She was so tired of trying to take care of herself. Would Kal want her to stay here if he knew how bad things were? And the baby. What would happen to him if she continued living here without help? After placing the drowsy infant in his crib,

Tela patted his back gently. She had to think about him, too. Looking down at her son, Tela made her decision.

Resolutely, Tela walked down the stairs and out to the yard. Waiting for her was breakfast. And a man with an offer. Looking into her eyes, Hawk searched for her answer.

Tela looked back boldly. "Yes, Mr. Hawk. I would like for you to take care of me and my baby."

Saying nothing, he motioned for her to sit and eat. They shared this meal in silence. He offered her a bottle of something. The stuff flowed sweetly between her lips. When she handed him the bottle back, his rough fingers closed gently over hers. His pale eyes spoke quietly to hers. He meant her no harm. A strange warmth burst free within her and spread throughout her body. His eyes spoke of protection, of a commitment to never leave her behind. She felt no fear for this man in the sun's morning light. In his pale eyes she saw what looked like comfort. She saw deliverance.

His first words to her were practical. "Where do you get water?"

"There's a well with a windmill," she said, pointing past the trees.

"The first thing I have to do for us is to find a place with water and food."

At Hawk's words, Kal's departure on a similar quest flashed painfully through her mind. The fear in her heart rose up into her eyes. Maybe she had been wrong. Maybe this man would leave and never return, too. Just like Kal.

Hawk sensed her sudden mood change. Kneeling beside her and lifting her chin to look into her eyes, he asked, "Is that why he left, to find water and food?"

"His name was Kal," she whispered. "He said he would come back for me. For us."

Hawk smiled at her. "Trust me, Tela. I'm tough. Like

you, I'm a survivor. Things are really bad out there. If Kal's been gone that long, he probably isn't … able to return. But whether I find a better place or not, I'll be back by sunset."

Tears made her eyes glitter. Tela knew Hawk almost said Kal was dead. Knowing her husband had loved her, Tela realized Kal's absence meant something had gone wrong. The lump this realization caused in her throat would not let her speak. Sensing her overpowering emotions, Hawk put the food inside the house and got ready to leave.

Tela listened until the bike's noise died in the distance. Unlike yesterday, the sound's fading brought no relief. Instead, the ensuing silence brought an intense feeling of being totally alone.

She moved through the day like a sleepwalker. Tomorrow, she'd be strong again. Today, she needed to hope that Hawk would return.

The sun slowly crawled across the sky. Shadows lengthened about the quiet house. The baby nursed and went to sleep, leaving Tela alone with the darkness and the silence. Stars glimmered against a velvet sky.

Tormented by old and new nightmares, she slept fitfully. In dreams she was young, lost in a terrifying storm. All around her, lightning flashed and thunder roared.

Awaking with a silent scream, Tela sat up, trembling, drenched with sweat. The nightmare ended, but the thunder continued. The sound was not rolling across the heavens but flying across the earth, promising something as precious as rain to her.

Looking over at the sleeping baby, Tela bounded out of bed and ran down the hall. Throwing open the front door, she saw bike and rider entering the dusty yard. Before Hawk could climb off the bike, she threw herself at him, nearly knocking him off balance.

"Hey, be careful!" he exclaimed. Her tear-damp cheek

pressed against his beard's roughness, her soft arms curved around his arms.

"I, I thought you weren't coming back," she sobbed against his neck.

"You'll find I keep my promises," he whispered. His mouth was warm against her forehead, his arm around her comforting and safe.

"I know that now," she murmured against his cheek. As their mouths found each other, words faded into soft, unintelligible comforts, lips gently returning caresses.

Hawk gently wrapped Tela's trembling body with his. Gently he covered her tear-wet cheeks with soft assurances. A low moan escaped her throat as the woman inside her resurrected. He swept her into his arms and carried her into the house.

The morning heat rose in the air with the sun. Tela stirred from peaceful sleep. Feeling Hawk's weight next to her, she snuggled in close, in spite of the warmth.

Too soon the baby stirred, fussing. Tela slowly crept from beneath Hawk's protective arm. Sitting on the foot of the bed, she let the baby nurse.

In a few minutes, the baby's purring woke Hawk. Crawling to sit behind her, he brushed his lips along her neck's soft nape. His whiskers pleasantly tickled her bare skin. The softness of his lips sent delicious sensations scurrying across her skin.

Looking over her shoulder at the baby, Hawk murmured, "I wish he was my son."

Smiling over her shoulder, Tela whispered, "I suppose he is yours now."

Hawk's rough hand traveled down the soft skin of her shoulder to the baby's downy head. "I guess he is, isn't he?"

"What will you do today?" she asked, almost afraid that

today would bring a repeat of yesterday's anxiety. She put the sleepy baby into his crib.

Hawk pulled her into the curve of his strong arms. Kissing her nose, he said, "Take you and our son to a better place. A place where there is plenty of water. Grass and trees and food."

Her eyes brightened. "Really? You found water already?"

"Lots of water," he replied. "It's the place the riders left."

A frown wrinkled her brow. "Will it be safe to go there?"

"That's what took me so long. I wanted to make sure they weren't coming back. There were no places near the lake left for them to raid. That's why Buskirk decided to pull out in the first place. All signs look like they've moved on for good."

Tela snuggled close to his muscled chest. "Lots of water? Enough to take a bath?"

"Yes, precious Tela," he chuckled. "Plenty to take a bath."

She hugged him. The molding of her soft body to his stirred the hunger in him. He looked down at her, questions in his eyes. She smiled as she kissed him, giving in gladly to the corresponding warmth spreading throughout her own body. Gone were pain and loneliness, melted by the warmth of Hawk's gentle caresses.

Later, Tela packed. There wasn't much to pack. A blanket, two quilts, cloths for diapers, the leftover food. On the back of the bike, Tela held the baby between her and Hawk to protect him from the wind and dust. He cried when the engine roared to life, but the machine's motion and Tela's gentle voice soon lulled the baby to sleep. Bundles securely tied to the bike, the baby contentedly snuggling in his mother's arms, Tela and Hawk began their journey to a better place.

The bike flew by ramshackled ruins. Once small towns, the abandoned buildings were dust's abode. The drought touched everything, town and country alike. The roadsides were dry and windswept as a desert. The countryside was empty, waiting, dying.

Long after the sun reached its zenith, Hawk slowed the bike. Scrubby, brown underbrush hid a dirt track from view. Turning down the track, they traveled on for a while. In the distance, Tela began to see trees, greenness! Hawk stopped the bike beside the porch of a small, rustic cabin.

Tela's eyes didn't see the cabin. Before her, peeking through trees, she saw a huge pool of shimmering water. She gasped in disbelief.

"Is it real?" she whispered.

Hawk chuckled. "As real as we are. There's a well behind the house with plenty of water, too. They must be fed by lots of deep springs to still be full in this drought."

"Who cares?" she laughed hysterically. "As long as the water's real!"

Her legs were numb from the long ride. Hawk helped her to stand. After untying the bundles, he disappeared into the cabin.

Tela stood where she dismounted, mesmerized by the expanse of water. Hawk came to the door and said, "Come see what I've done for the baby."

Tela reluctantly entered the small house. Hawk tied ropes and the blanket to make a hammock bed for the baby.

"See if he likes it," Hawk said, after Tela had fed and changed the baby.

Tela laid the contented infant on top of the tightly folded quilt, the blanket's edges curling around the quilt to form a cocoon. The hammock swayed gently back and forth. Sighing, the baby drifted into untroubled slumber.

"I think he loves it," she whispered, putting her arms around Hawk's neck.

Nibbling her ear, Hawk asked, "How about that bath?"

"The baby!" Tela protested.

"I'll stay close enough to hear him if he cries. You go first."

Tela peeled off clothes and laid them at the water's edge. The wetness closed coldly around her warm flesh. She gasped, losing her breath. When she finally felt clean, she retrieved her clothes and scrubbed them in the water, too. Unashamedly, she walked naked back to the cabin, wet clothes in her hands. As she draped her wet clothes over the porch's railing, Hawk teasingly slapped her rear and headed to the lake for his own bath.

Darkness fell softly around the cabin. Hawk snared and dressed a rabbit. It was thin, only a few mouthfuls, but cooked over the fire, the meat was a feast. Appearing in the sky, stars rained down cool, white light from cloudless heavens. A yellow moon peeked out from behind the trees. Lazily, Tela stretched in the night's peacefulness.

Hawk paused in his chatter to the cooing baby. He looked at Tela as she stretched. She smiled.

"You've never told me his name," Hawk said.

Tela answered, "I never named him. I kept waiting for Kal to come back."

Hawk looked at the baby. "We can't have that, can we, little man? You need a name."

Tela looked thoughtfully into the night sky. Smiling, she said, "What about Adam? And after his real father. How about Adam Kal Hawk? 'The first' and the son of two."

Hawk looked at the baby. "Adam Kal Hawk – do you like that name, little man?"

The infant gurgled happily, punching Hawk's bearded cheeks with his tiny fists. "I think he approves, Mama."

A happy mist filled Tela's eyes.

Sometime in the night, Tela stirred from pleasant dreams. In the distance, she heard a low, menacing rumble. Suddenly wide awake, she turned to wake Hawk. The riders were coming back! But the bed beside her was empty. "Hawk?" she whispered into the dark.

"Out here, Tela," his voice, deep and melodic, caressed her name.

Tela saw his outline in the night. He faced the west. Slipping her arm around him, she asked, "Does that sound mean the riders are coming back?"

Kissing her furrowed brow, Hawk smiled. "No, my precious Tela. Look over there."

She looked at the sky where Hawk pointed. In a second, brilliant fingers of light danced across low, dark clouds. They watched as black, boiling pillars of fire and accompanying rumbles of thunder chased each other across the sky. Greedily swallowing the stars, the clouds ravaged the quiet heavens.

Then the smell of a storm, ozone from the lightning, filled their nostrils. The rain began to fall, diamond droplets pouring liquid onto the tortured earth. The dust soaked up the sweet wetness. Then the clouds burst. Cascading rain forced Hawk and Tela to the cabin's porch. Hissing steam from the hot earth swirled upward around them.

During the lightning flashes, Tela gazed into Hawk's clear, piercing eyes. He wrapped his arms around her slender frame tightly. As he looked at the heavens, Hawk's strong face glowed with a gratitude for the salvation of second chances. Pulled close against his chest, Tela smelled damp leather and the scent of a man.

Tela whispered, "It's all over now, isn't it, Hawk? It's finally all over."

Hawk tilted her face up with his fingers to look into her eyes. Hope flowed from him to engulf her. Against the backdrop sounds of nature's miracle, Hawk's voice whispered deep and melodic against her mouth, "On the contrary, my precious one. Everything's just begun."

Balance

Stars bleed.
Clouds cry.
Leaves parch,
Men die.

Stones speak.
Rain sings.
Men give.
Life brings.

Buried Treasure

In all of my searching and aimless excursions,
Among the unconscious, wild seeds I had sown,
Within me, unnoticed and patiently waiting,
Was the person I wanted to become all along.

Butterfly

Gone the bright energy of spring.
Autumn's breath rests 'neath your wing.
Bit of a rainbow, fly to the moon.
Winter's chill is coming soon.

HIDDEN ANSWER

Life sang forth her glorious song,
Warmth, beauty, light.
Darkness came to sing his dirge,
Death, cold, night.

Soon darkness's dreary song ended,
Surrendered to love's chant.
Love's sweet song helped me to find
What a true life really meant.

IMMIGRANT

Tired feet, aching heads,
Empty stomachs,
Searching minds, extended hands.
Tear-filled eyes,
Pain-filled hearts.

Hollowed cheeks, dry-mouthed words,
Longing, sadness,
Searching minds, extended hands.
Mournful days,
Closing darkness.

A long, empty tunnel.
No guiding hands,
No caring hearts.

Into The Light

Death's face looks down
The narrow corridor of light,
Searching for a waiting soul.
Her mouth is wide open,
Her eyes are shut tight,
She calls but sees not who goes.

Those answer who dwell
In the darkness of pain
Hearing Death call mournfully.
They hear and follow
Never to roam again.
Not speaking, they go, and they see.

MELODY

Hearken to the song of life,
The song of love, of joy, of strife.
Hear it echo in life's hall.
Hearken to it one and all.

Hear of love from bygone days.
Hear love sung in many ways.
As love is sung, know and weep
For the things you cannot keep.

Hear of joy as full and true
As the day it came to you.
Hear and want joy as it's sung,
Joy ever anew, like bells, rung.

Hear of strife, but don't give in,
It's the downfall of good men.
Enjoy life, and join its song,
May your tune be sweet and long.

Note In A Bottle

Things came together in my world's corner,
Melody, laughter, love.

I shared them with the trees
Who shook their leaves
Into a mirrored pool.

All the water's excess
Ran into a subterranean stream
To carry my secrets to another

Who sat by that stream
To dream.

MEMORIES

A hot, southwest wind blew relentlessly, stirring up dust devils. Slowly the tiny cyclones collapsed, covering every surface with powder. Humid air lay heavily against my skin. At my feet on the dusty porch, Matthew played, oblivious to the humidity, the dust, and the hellish heat. Dabbing my forehead with my handkerchief, I marveled at the innocent acceptance of childhood.

The persistent heat and lack of rain made the main road into Franklinton a cracked puzzle. No one moved in the midday heat. Two hundred yards past my driveway, Mr. Steele walked out on his store's porch. Mopping his neck with a red bandana, he gave a disappointed look to the turquoise sky.

The sky held no deliverance from the heat, just like the past months held no deliverance for me. Wiping perspiration from my own brow, I wished I had to worry about William being out in the sun-baked fields. But I didn't today or any other day. Tired from the heat and from too many memories, I looked down at my son. "Matthew, let's walk to the store for a coke."

William's eyes looked up at me from Matthew's sweet face. "Oh, could we, Mommie? Oh, boy!" He scurried to gather up his toys.

I needed more than a cold drink. I needed to escape the house's quietness. I needed to escape from thinking. To escape from painful memories.

Taking twenty cents from my purse, I closed the wooden door. Matthew threaded his tiny fingers through mine and pulled me down the steps into the sweltering sunshine.

"Howdy, Mrs. Anderson," Mr. Steele greeted us with a tired smile. "What can I do for you folks today?"

I returned his smile with a tired one of my own. "We'd like a couple of colas, please, Mr. Steele." Eager for his treat, Matthew ran to climb up on a stool at the counter.

The soda's cool fizz slid down my throat. "Have you heard when this weather will let up?"

Mr. Steele wiped his bald head. "No time soon, I'm afraid."

Outside a delivery van rattled down the road and slid to a stop in front of the store. Through the window and dust, I read letters on the vehicle, "Yaloshuba County Correctional Institution." Weather-beaten buildings and high fences flashed in my mind. Memories of the prison made me shiver even in the heat. William took me with him once when he worked for a time with prison ministries. I didn't have the constitution for a second visit.

An officer from the prison strolled through the door. I recognized her from Mary Jane Hill's description. Mary Jane and her husband, Joe, worked with William at the prison every Sunday for three months. They passed out tracts and New Testaments to inmates who possessed a modicum of sanity. Mary Jane described all the guards to me, especially Clytee Bertram, in great detail. I recognized Officer Bertram the instant she walked into Mr. Steele's store. Mary Jane also told me Officer Bertram was as mean as a snake and mistreated the inmates in her charge.

Closely behind Officer Bertram trailed a pathetically

thin woman clothed in a gray prison uniform. Behind the two women loped a huge man, so tall he stooped to enter the store, so wide he dwarfed the store's interior. He wore the same dismal uniform as the woman.

Matthew stared in fascination, soda forgotten, straw hanging limply between his lips. I couldn't stop staring either, partly from shock the county allowed two prisoners outside, partly at the sight of such a giant man. An uneasy feeling grabbed my insides. Tiny hairs on the back of my neck prickled.

"Matthew, honey, finish your cola. It's time to go," I smiled, hoping my anxiety didn't show.

Matthew never took his eyes off the giant. In the too loud voice of an innocent, he asked, "Mommie, who is that man?"

Giving him my best be-quiet-because-you're-in church glare, I helped him down from the stool. "It's time to go, baby. Tell Mr. Steele how much you enjoyed your cola."

"Thanks for the coke, Mr. Steele!" Matthew called, waving over his shoulder.

When we passed the man, I looked into his face. I expected the same glassy expression as in the female prisoner's eyes. Instead, his eyes spoke to me. Intelligence looked out through sadness. Surprised, I dropped my gaze and hurried out the door.

Those haunting eyes stirred strange emotions in me. Back on the porch, I couldn't forget the pain I saw in them. His eyes reminded me of what I saw every time I looked in the mirror. Surrounded on the porch by his toys, Matthew soon forgot the man. As I opened both wooden doors on the front porch, I couldn't get those eyes out of my mind.

My thoughts ricocheted back to William. Too much in love to wait, we married the weekend after high school graduation. Generational farmers, William's family gave us two hundred acres of fertile land and a small house on the main thoroughfare into town as a wedding gift. The end of our first year together blessed us. The fields provided abundant crops, markets paid good prices, and we were expecting our first child.

Five years later, the spring and early summer blasted the fields with unusual heat. Trying to save the crops, William spent long hours in the fields with new irrigation rigs. He came home too tired to eat, too worried to play with Matthew, too depressed to spend time with me. One afternoon, William didn't come home at all. At supper time, I walked to Mr. Steele's store and called my father-in-law to help me find William. At twilight, Papa Anderson's men found William face down in the dirt he loved. He'd suffered a heat stroke, the doctor said.

By midnight, I was a widow. No loud whistling woke me in the morning, no cheerful singing told me to put supper on the table in the evenings. Muddy field boots waited quietly by the back door. Happy days filled with laughter and love turned into long hours of solitude haunted by memories. William's death knocked my existence askew, teetering me unevenly on pain's pivot.

Thank goodness, Matthew anchored me! His singsong voice and little boy energy kept me from losing my mind. Like many afternoons, I settled myself in the porch rocker to eavesdrop on his play.

My eyes wandered down the road to Mr. Steele's store. The prisoners carried box after box of supplies and stowed them in the van. When the woman prisoner passed the giant, she looked up at him and offered a pitiful smile.

After a while, I heard Officer Bertram's loud voice, "Well, I reckon that's all we need fer now, Steele. Much obliged t'ya. See ya next month."

Officer Bertram walked out of the store, the prisoners

following closely behind. The man deposited a final box in the back of the van. Moving to the open side door, he placed his hand on the roof and foot on the running board. For a moment he hesitated, looking over the vehicle's roof at the officer.

Loudly, Bertram barked, "Well, g'on, Thompkins. Get in!"

The man slowly shook his massive head. "I ain't goin' back."

"Don't be silly, Thompkins," the officer laughed, her cheeks turning scarlet, from either emotion or maybe just from the heat. "Get in. You got no choice."

The woman prisoner moved to stand beside him. She plucked his sleeve with nervous fingers. "C'mon, Jesse. Us got t'go now." Her high pitched voice mimicked a scared child's whine.

The man jerked his arm away from the woman's touch. Shaking his head again, he put both feet on the ground and shut the door. From somewhere Officer Bertram pulled out a pistol. Waving it toward the obstinate man, she bellowed, "Don't want t'have t'use this, Jesse, boy. Now get in the truck!"

Something in the man's posture changed. For a moment I thought he gave in. "Rather die than go back t' 'at hell-hole. No, ma'am, I ain't goin' back."

The air hummed with tension. Officer Bertram's red face, the obstinate inmate, and the waving pistol made me scoop up Matthew and hurry him inside. The sadness and tragedy hanging around in my lonely house expanded like fog to permeate the outside air. Fear threaded the air, too, an uneasy premonition, like nut grass strands on bare feet. I knew I should stay inside with Matthew, but the emotions pulled me back outside.

By the time I got to the porch, premonition became

reality. The man ran toward my yard. A fire flash spat from the end of the pistol. Suspended momentarily, the man's body arced against the cloudless sky then tumbled to the yard's dry grass. In my ears drummed the shot's thunder and my heart's beating.

With a will of their own my feet carried me to the gray-clad man bleeding his life away in my yard. His chest moved up and down rapidly. I looked up the street for help. Mr. Steele came outside his store. "Call a doctor!" I yelled to him. I pointed at the officer and shouted, "And keep that blood-thirsty creature out of my yard!"

The helpless feeling I had sitting beside William while he took his last breaths flooded my mind. I begged God through those short hours to let my husband open his eyes just once so I could tell him I loved him. If I could tell him I loved him, maybe he would fight harder.

William never regained consciousness. I buried him near the edge of the fields he loved. The fields that took him from me.

This wounded man bleeding in my yard had his eyes wide open. He looked up at me. Overwhelming emotions shook my legs and knocked me to the ground beside him.

For some reason, I pulled his shaggy head onto my lap. The elevation helped his breathing some. Thousands of thoughts ran through my mind. How could someone so deliberately and carelessly choose to end his life? Surely he knew what would happen. Perhaps he really was insane. Maybe in the store, I mistook momentary lucidity for sanity when I looked into his eyes.

I looked at his face. The blue eyes looking up into mine were as sane as my own. Tears blurred my vision.

"It's alright, ma'am. It's alright. I didn' b'long there with th' others. They'd never've let me leave any other way. Don't you fret none."

"How can you say that?" I asked, my respect for life aghast at his willingness to die.

"She was so pretty, ma'am, just like you," he coughed, a faraway look stealing across his ragged face. "I'll never forget the first time I saw her runnin' down the road, coal black hair a-flyin' full b'hind her like a horse's mane. She had laughin' eyes, a china doll face. Couldn' b'lieve it when she said she'd marry me. Thought I's the luckiest man in th' whole world."

An old sadness filled his eyes with tears. His cheeks grew paler by the second. His efforts to speak took their toll on his strength.

"Came home one day from work t' find her packin'. 'Jesse,' says she, 'Did ya really think a small-town hick nobody like you could keep me forever?' She'd met another man, a travelin' salesman. He promised her the moon, and she b'lieved he could deliver. She was runnin' off."

He fought to share his story. "She laughed and laughed at me, callin' me country bumpkin, no good, all kinds of hurtful names. Somethin' inside me made me grab her. I started shakin' her, screamin' at her to stop. I yelled t' drown out th' wicked sound of her laugh."

Huge tears slid from the corners of his eyes into the gray at his temples. "Shook her too hard, I reckon. Pretty head was just rollin' 'round on that thin little neck of hers."

With a sob, he whispered, "She didn't laugh at me no more."

"When I come to my senses, I was locked up with all those crazy people. Guess I was crazy at first, wantin' to feel her in my arms, callin' out her name, even when I was awake. Didn' know she was dead 'til the officers told me so."

He gasped, his breath rattling in his chest. He opened

his eyes wide. This time I saw fear in them. "Ma'am, d' ya know the twenty-third Psalm?"

I nodded.

"My ma always used t' say it t' me at night when I was little and afraid of the dark. It's getting' kinda dark now, and I'm afraid. Please, would ya say it t' me?"

I cleared my throat and shakily began. "The Lord is my Shepherd, I shall not want…"

The man's hand flailed upward as if searching for something to hold to. I wrapped my fingers around his and placed our hands over his heart. His fingers were colder than the cola I drank this morning. How long ago? An eternity. Minutes seemed like hours.

"He maketh me to lie down in green pastures. He leadeth me beside the still waters. He restoreth my soul. He leadeth me in the paths of righteousness for his name's sake. Yea, though I walk through the valley of the shadow of death, I will fear no evil… ."

Silently, the man mouthed the psalm with me. A peace settled on his ragged face. The lump in my throat grew too big for me to continue. Hot tears rolled down my cheeks.

He looked up at me and smiled. "Thanks, ma'am. That's the part I wanted to hear." His body shook convulsively. He closed his eyes, whispering, "Fear no evil… ." He coughed, his breath escaping from deep in his chest, and then he was still.

I don't know how long I sat staring into Jesse Thompkin's peaceful face. When I looked up, people lined the edge of my front yard. Matthew stood beside me, his tiny hand on my shoulder.

For the first time I didn't say anything to explain to Matthew what he had witnessed. The year before, my baby repeated thousands of times to friends and family, "My daddy's gone to live with the angels." He understood as much as any young child could about death. Questions about today would come.

What my neighbors or in-laws would think or say never crossed my mind. I sat in my front yard in broad daylight holding the head of a convict in my lap as if he had been a lifelong friend. In those dreamlike moments, suffering and kindness struggled. Jesse Thompkins was a human being who owned the right to some dignity and to a kind touch while facing death.

When Jesse died, his last moments mirrored the reflection of my weaknesses and strengths. In the days that followed, I realized things about myself that I had not when William died. One thing I didn't feel at all for Jesse was pity. In his death he found peace. Somewhere in space and time, Jesse Thompkins was free from painful memories. He made a choice to be free. Not a very good way to choose freedom, but he had decided. His courage to make a difficult decision gave me courage to choose. Life continued without William, and so must I. Not with the pain of my memories, but with their joys.

For all my days, whenever my courage ebbed, or life's circumstances proved difficult, in my mind I heard Jesse's final whispered words, "Fear no evil."

POSSIBILITY

Worlds in a never ending procession
Down space's corridors,
Unexplored vastness
Unencumbered by man or beast.

Worlds free from every vice
Full of promise.

Worlds alone, spinning, waiting.

REQUEST

Waves crash to shore
Tumbling castles. A gull calls.
Inside me, walls tumble.
Time's sands beat them down.
New dreams, just born,
Struggle to exist, with
Feelings far different
From those under time's fall.
I long to draw the cloak
Of childish innocence
About my shoulders.
In my hands, the faded robe
Turns to tatters.
Future throws the familiar rags
Back into Past's dark face.
Future hands me a new robe,
One that's far too large.
Escaping from beneath time's sands,
Yesterday's dreams race backward
To bring another innocent
Into the future.
Flee quickly, dreams,
To Past's netherworld.
Guide well steps not yet born into the present
And, please, be kinder.

SHIELD

Tears and weakness, side by side,
Burning tears I try to hide.
Searing pain behind my eyes,
Strength to shield what boils inside.

Vulnerable am I without strength's shield.
Emotions conquer, their persuasions wield
Pain. Eyes and heart completely filled,
Too weak to fight, to tears I yield.

Emotions flow to outer paths –
Woes and pains and hurts and wraths.
Sweet release, a cleansing bath
My soul trembles, tears' aftermath.

Once again, strength's shield I raise,
Remembering the tempest's tearful haze,
On to face life's other days
Full of faith and hope and praise.

SOMEWHERE

Through my night window
A yellow moon burns a hole in the velvet sky.

Somewhere,
Rainforests disappear,
Animals die.

Here,
The stars number thousands,
Untouched by man.

Through my night window
A soft, cool breeze blows into my quiet room.

Somewhere,
Crops wither.
People starve.

Here,
Crickets sing symphonies
Predicting rain.

Tapestry

Deserted lake shores,
Grass in the wind,
Rain falling soundlessly,
Silver, golden days.

Silver and golden days
Woven amid plain, brown threads,
Life's tapestry resplendent
With silver, golden days.

Contentment in a gentle touch,
Love from a soft, lingering caress,
Halcyon days exist, a haven,
Autumn's silver, golden days.

The Romance Of Spring And Winter

Quiet as a baby sleeping, Winter tiptoes away.
Spring meets and hails him in her colorful array.

Winter hesitates in Spring's embrace,
Yellow, azure, lilac -- trees in budding lace.

Grass pushes through fertile brown to kiss the couple's feet
Miraculous birth of nature, when Spring and Winter
    meet!

TRUTH

As time passes, I realize
Life's not always as it seems.
Picture books and fairy tales
Come true in plays and dreams.

There are no castles in the clouds,
No charming prince will come.
Fantasies fall down to earth.
Princesses must stay home.

Wisdom

I still enjoy laughter,
The fragrance of a flower,
A hand's warm pressure
On mine.

My body is old.
My mind is not.
The experiences I can share
Don't ignore.

I feel joy and sadness.
I know pain and gladness.
Give me a little of yourself,
And I'll show you the world.

PLACES

After looking at her from head to toe, the man across the aisle stared, like she'd been teleported to the spot from a distant planet. Camilla smiled. Perhaps New York fashions were a bit much for a bus trip along a Mississippi highway.

Bradleyville. How long since she had been home? Three years? The computer kept her parents in touch, but her career kept her in New York. In less than an hour, Camilla would be home. Her special place.

The bus crawled past a new service station. With air brakes whooshing, the bus stopped in front of the tiny depot next door.

In front of the station's shiny pumps sat a battered pickup truck. Against the truck's side leaned a tall man. A closely trimmed beard decorated his square jaw. Light curls topped his head in contrast to the red of his beard. Scanning a newspaper while his truck's tank filled, the man was totally oblivious to Camilla's scrutiny. Something in his muscled body's relaxed slouch mirrored the relaxed calm she always felt in this place. Bradleyville. Home. Camilla exhaled slowly.

Her interest in the stranger surprised Camilla. She smiled, thinking of her roommate, Lucy. Lucy, the liberal, reared in Boston's high society. In spite of Camilla's conservative upbringing in tiny Bradleyville, friendship had blossomed between the two. Common careers and goals cemented the bond. The only contention between them existed in affairs of the heart. Lucy insisted on finding dates for Camilla and bringing her along to every function. Camilla protested, longing for privacy and quietness after long days of modeling. Slightly antisocial, Camilla chose to put love and all its trappings on hold for her career. Lucy, the opposite, floated around New York's socialite scene, usually on the arm of some fabulous man. Camilla smiled as she thought of how surprised Lucy would be if she could see Camilla staring at the handsome stranger.

Inside the depot, Camilla borrowed the phone book and used her cell. In less than three minutes, Mr. Hankins drove up in his spotless '79 Oldsmobile. The only cab in Bradleyville, Mr. Hankins prided himself on quick service.

Consistency. That was something Camilla missed most in the past three years. In New York Camilla tried not to change too much, especially at first. Eventually the impetuous city captured her and swirled her from shoot to shoot and through the entire melee between. Camilla slowly felt the genuineness of a girl from the south changing into a jaded New Yorker.

Except for dating. Camilla guarded her private life closely, selfishly. She and Lucy forever fought over Camilla's self-imposed censorship of her social life.

"How on earth do you ever expect to meet Mr. Right if you don't let me introduce you to a few Mr. Wrongs?" Lucy wailed. She had arranged a meeting for Camilla with a very eligible lawyer.

Recalling clearly the fiasco date Lucy arranged for her two weeks prior, Camilla flatly refused.

"I'm not accepting tonight, Lucy," Camilla answered,

smiling sweetly. "You know I'm too busy right now for a man in my life."

"Gosh, I'm not talking about lifetime commitments, Cam," Lucy frowned. "Just one date can't be that bad. Besides, Jeff is sooooo yummy!"

"You can't judge a book by its cover," Camilla sighed. Heading toward her bedroom with an unfinished novel in her hand, she added, "Like this one. It's sooooo boring, and the cover looked sooooo promising."

"You know you're going to die an old maid," Lucy harrumphed at Camilla's retreating back. Picking up her cell, Lucy dialed Jeff to let him know Camilla would not be meeting him for dinner.

"Well, Camilla Bradford!" exclaimed Mr. Hankins, helping Camilla put her suitcase in the cab. "Girl, I almost didn't recognize you."

Camilla smiled. Like the man on the bus, Mr. Hankins stared at her outfit. Casually Camilla asked him about his family. Her outside might look different, but inside she was still the same small town girl. Put at ease by Camilla's smiles and questions, Mr. Hankins chattered about his grandchildren all the way to the Bradford's house.

When the cab started to turn between the twin rows of oaks at the end of the Bradford's drive, Camilla touched Mr. Hankins' shoulder. "Would you mind stopping here, Mr. Hankins? I want to surprise Mom and Dad."

"Sure," he chuckled. "Can I help you with your suitcase?"

"I can manage, thanks," Camilla smiled.

Mr. Hankins waved the money she offered him away. "On the house," he smiled. "Welcome home. It's been good seeing you again."

Slowly Camilla walked up the drive, her new boots shuffling through the bright yellows and reds of fallen leaves.

The long drive was exactly like the picture in her mind she had seen so many times over the past three years. Happy tears made her eyes glisten.

"Hey, anybody home?" she called.

When Camilla stepped onto the porch, her parents burst from the house. Showering her with hugs and kisses, they both talked at once. The past three years had etched new lines on her parents' strong faces. Those tiny lines tugged at Camilla's heart. She needed to visit home more often. At least once a year.

The next morning, Camilla woke to tantalizing odors. She stretched like a cat before a December fire. A day of uninterrupted leisure! No heavy makeup, no flashing lights, no attempts to capture her essence on an eight by ten glossy. Slipping on a robe, she padded softly down the hall's hardwood toward the food smells.

Her mother looked up from the stove. "Good mornin', sleepyhead. Rest well?"

"Like a log," Camilla yawned. "What time is it?"

"Almost nine," her father chuckled. "I see you still like to sleep late. At least some things haven't changed."

Camilla gave him a bear hug and kissed the tip of his nose. "I'll always be your little girl on the inside," she teased. "No matter how much changes on the outside."

A smile stretched across his face. "Good to have you home, honey bee," he said.

"Good to be home, Daddy," she smiled back, sitting down to the steaming plate her mother set before her.

Camilla smothered a hot, buttered biscuit with pear preserves. Their sweetness lay richly on her tongue, stirring childhood memories. Between delicious mouthfuls, she asked, "Do my two streams still flow down in the hollow?"

Busily scrubbing an iron skillet, her mother answered over her shoulder, "I think so, baby."

"Now, Mother, someone bought the McCleary place from the kids when Zeke died," her father reminded. To Camilla he added, "Some Yankee artist fellow. I heard in town he dammed up the streams to build a lake. Kept hearing machinery down there when he first moved in. Don't expect anything's the same in the hollow now. I haven't walked down to look."

Camilla detected an antagonistic tone in her father's Southern drawl. Not a hypocrite about his dislike for Yankees, her father warned her when she left for a career in New York about Northerners and about their love for constantly changing things. Camilla knew firsthand her father's ideas were skewed. The changes Northerners' made weren't just for the sake of change. To attempt to convince her father of that would be hopeless. He hated changing anything, especially his mind.

Finishing breakfast, Camilla remembered every detail of her special place in the woods. Two springs rose from the earth, converged into a pool, and emptied into one creek that ran down the hollow. Between the two springs' heads lay a moss-covered peninsula. Camilla claimed the peninsula as hers when she was a very young girl. The property belonged to the McClearys, not to the Bradfords. Friends of her parents, the McClearys hadn't minded Camilla's presence in the hollow. She spent many lazy afternoons under the spreading oaks, dreaming, reading books, and listening to the water's gurgles.

If the artist had dammed the streams, her special place was gone forever. One unexpected change.

In her room, Camilla shed her robe, donned jeans and a flannel shirt, and slipped on sneakers. Running manicured nails through auburn curls, she studied the face in the mirror. A complexion as flawless as cream, a nose flared a little too much at the nostrils, and eyes that couldn't decide exactly what color to be. The face belonged to a woman, not to a dreamy-eyed girl.

"Not too old for jeans, sneakers, and a romp through the woods, though," Camilla said aloud to her reflection.

Peeking through the doorway, Camilla called to her parents in the family room, "I'm going out for a walk. Be back in a while."

"Be careful, honey bee. Watch for snakes."

"I will. And yes, I have my phone in my pocket."

The familiar warning her parents used time and again when she was younger now made Camilla wonder if her cautiousness with men were somehow connected. After all, some of the men she dated had been snake-like! Not that Camilla didn't enjoy being friends with men. Like her friendship with Jake. Jake shot pictures for Bon Genre, the company for which she modeled. He, Lucy, and Camilla had great fun together. But a date with a man was different. Being alone together, especially for the first time, always made Camilla uncomfortable. She worried she would say or do the wrong thing, worried the guy might get too friendly too fast, worried about the inevitable feelings of rejection when the guy never called for a second date.

After a few arranged dates that more than substantiated her opinion of disaster, Camilla decided to concentrate on her career. Leave the affairs of the heart to the pros. Like Lucy.

Temptingly cool air met Camilla at the wood's outer perimeter. The oaks were shedding their leaves, pointing their branches up to an azure sky. Fallen leaves and damp soil filled her nostrils with the smells of fall. No taxi horns or emergency vehicle sounds filled the air, no impatient bodies jostled her on a crowded sidewalk. Simply the muted symphony of life hummed around her.

Wouldn't Lucy be out of place here, without the noise, the parties, and the stores to frequent? Camilla could hear Lucy, "Oh, Cam! How dreadfully boring! Give me New York any day!"

Camilla loved New York-- the glamour, the bustle, the people, but today, the cool touch of clean air felt good against her cheeks.

Camilla searched along the forest floor for the neglected path leading down to her streams. Eventually she discovered the path lying barely visible beneath the tangled underbrush. She picked her way carefully among the brambles until finally she reached the ridge overlooking her special place.

For a moment Camilla was afraid to look. When her hazel eyes looked down into the hollow, joy leaped within her. Except for the sparkling new lake beyond, the hollow looked completely unchanged. The autumn sun filtered through bare limbs and cast diamond spangles of light on the water. The two gurgling streams danced into the same small pool and then poured over a new rock wall into the lake. All along the streams lay emerald moss, spreading like a carpet on the forest floor.

Like one trapped in a special moment, Camilla became that little girl discoverer who had originally found the beauty of this enchanted place. Elated, she bounded down the ridge, pulling off her sneakers so the soft moss caressed her bare feet. Hugging herself, a shoe in each hand, she spun around with childish glee. Laughing, she felt the relief of one who'd lost something infinitely precious only to unexpectedly rediscover it.

Dizzy and ecstatic, Camilla sat down beside her shoes on the peninsula. Her eyes followed the silvery thread of a snail's trail across the moss.

Suddenly on the pond's opposite side, almost hidden by the trees, Camilla saw a figure. Tall and broad, the body loomed, the form almost lost in the shadows.

Camilla felt fear creep in. Her New York wariness for strangers caused her to bounce to her feet.

As she turned to leave, a deep voice called to her, "Please don't go."

She turned around. The man stepped forward into the light. The sun played fully on his face. She recognized the square jaw covered with a red beard, saw gentle laugh lines etched around his eyes and mouth, saw wheat-colored curls. The stranger she'd seen at the service station on the highway!

Above a straight nose, his eyes looked into hers. Their clear blueness held no threat. Camilla relaxed and looked down at her bare feet.

"I seem to have forgotten something anyway."

The man smiled. "Didn't you know all nymphs walk the forest in bare feet?"

"Is that so?" she smiled back. "You must be the Yank, er, the artist that bought the McCleary place?"

"That's me," he laughed, deep and warm. "And you must be Mr. Bradford's famous daughter."

Camilla blushed, wondering what this man had heard about her. "I'm Camilla Bradford."

"My name's Eric. Eric Hansen."

For the first time, Camilla noticed an easel standing in the shadows behind the man. Gesturing toward the canvas, Eric asked, "Mind if I paint you in?"

Camilla looked down at her jeans. "Like this?"

"You look perfect."

That night, Eric ate supper with the Bradfords. Camilla had impulsively invited him, and her hospitable mother wasn't upset in the slightest. Camilla's parents liked Eric right away. Even her Yankee-phobic father quickly warmed to the artist, talking to him about everyday things as if they were lifelong friends.

After supper, Camilla and Eric sat out in the porch swing and shared a laugh about some funny story Mr. Bradford had told earlier. If Lucy could only see her now! Camilla, the girl destined to be an old maid, laughing on a porch swing with a handsome stranger!

The next morning Eric called Camilla. "I thought you might like to see some of my work."

Camilla hesitated. "I would like to see your work, but..." Her words trailed off as she tried to make an excuse. She had come home to rest. An interlude with a handsome stranger was far from what Camilla had planned.

"I promise to be a perfect gentleman," Eric added.

Smiling, Camilla replied, "In that case, I'd love to see some of your work."

"Be there to get you in about five minutes."

"Let me walk over. I love the woods this time of year."

The McCleary house was a rustic structure with a spacious interior. Eric led Camilla around the old house and showed her his work filling the walls of the first floor rooms.

Impressed with his brush techniques, Camilla asked, "Have you ever sold any?" The intricacies of a forest at sunset painting fascinated her.

"A few years ago I sold some to a dealer from New York. An exhibitor wanted me to bring up enough for a show, but I'd gotten used to my life here. I told him thanks but no thanks."

Camilla shook her pretty head. "Seems such a waste to keep them tucked away here where no one can enjoy them."

"Oh, I sell a few to local people," Eric said. "That's enough for me."

"Don't you ever want your work to be recognized by professionals?" she asked, knowing how good she felt when a stranger occasionally whispered behind her back, "That's Camilla Bradford."

"Not really," he answered truthfully. "I have no desire to be famous. I enjoy painting. I don't ever want my work to be just for money or for egotistical reasons."

"Then, how do you live?" Camilla looked around the comfortably furnished house. "None of my business, but you do have bills to pay?"

He nodded, "I do small repair jobs around town sometimes. I like using my hands to fix things. My parents left me some money when they died, and I've made a few good investments here and there. I manage. I don't need much. I'm happy with a simple life."

Camilla peeked sideways at him from under long lashes. He intrigued her, this man who demanded little from life. His unassuming manner knocked repeatedly against the wall she had carefully built to protect her inner self. For the first time she wondered what she had missed by avoiding all serious relationships with men.

This man intrigued her. Underneath Eric's quiet exterior, Camilla sensed a controlled strength. There was much more to him than met the eye. Of course, she couldn't help but notice the physical strength in his muscled body. Her staid resistance to Lucy's constant let-me-fix-you-up-with attitude began to melt.

Returning to New York might be a bit less exciting this time.

During all the days of Camilla's three week vacation she shared with him, Eric never made any romantic advances toward Camilla. She surprised herself by wishing he would!

She hoped she detected a faint tenderness in his eyes sometimes when he looked at her. He seemed comfortably content to just be in her company.

One morning three days before the end of her vacation, Camilla packed a lunch for them. Loading the picnic basket in the back of Eric's truck, the two drove to a nearby park where they hiked, laughed, and talked. On the way home, Camilla asked Eric if he would ever reconsider the art exhibitor's offer.

Eric stared silently out the windshield at the darkening highway. Raking his fingers through his hair, he answered, "I'm definitely not anxious to go back to a big city like New York. People in big cities have a tendency to step on other people to get what they want. I don't particularly enjoy watching that happen. Or having it happen to me."

"There are lots of decent folks in big cities, too," Camilla protested, thinking of Lucy, Jake, and her other friends. "You can't lump everybody into one category. It's not fair."

"You're right, I suppose. I've found out, though, that not much in life is fair. I've been in too many bad situations to risk repetitions."

Camilla persisted, "You can't hide out in the woods forever. You're missing things. Good stuff."

Eric shook his head. "I'm content with my cabin, my repair work, and my painting. Maybe someday I'll change. For now, I'm happy the way things are."

They rode the rest of the way in silence. Camilla thought Eric must have been hurt terribly in the past to want to hide away in the cabin's solitude. Certainly nothing she said could change his mind.

A thought came slithering unexpectedly into Camilla's mind. She had been doing the same thing as Eric. She had hidden from relationships for fear of being hurt. She didn't start relationships because of the risk of relationships ending. Suddenly Eric's stubborn staying in the country made sense. Only something miraculous could change such deep-seated convictions. Still, the part of her life Camilla chose to protect from the public affected no one except her. Because of Eric's decision, his beautiful artwork would be undiscovered.

The days of Camilla's vacation passed too quickly. Not certain how to tell Eric she was leaving, not certain if she should say anything at all except goodbye, Camilla put off telling him about her scheduled departure until the day before she left.

Dialing his number on her cell, Camilla waited for Eric to answer.

"Eric, can I come over for a short while?"

"I was about to call you. I finished something I want you to see."

Camilla pulled on a down jacket as she left the empty house. Her parents had gone out to eat with some friends. Camilla had stayed home alone to relax. The house's emptiness echoed the emptiness growing in Camilla over saying goodbye to her family and to this place tomorrow.

Outside the house, the wind rose with the sun's descent. The air's chill seeped through her warm clothing. The flashlight in her hand gave off light but no warmth. Above her head, bare tree limbs creaked a melancholy melody, appropriate background music for her solitary journey across the streams.

Before Camilla knocked, Eric opened the door. His eyes sparkled. He pulled her in to warm by a crackling fire.

Shedding her jacket, Camilla knelt to warm her hands at the cheerful blaze. The fire heated her cold cheeks, turning them from pink to rosy red. The smoke and light made her eyes smart, causing moisture to brighten their depths. Her mind sought for the right words to say to Eric. She didn't want guarded emotions to escape into words.

Camilla vowed years ago to never invest this much emotion in any relationship, at least not at this particular time in her life. Yet without realizing, she allowed this gentle man to stroll into secret places in her mind and heart. The return to her career tomorrow would force her to leave behind more than home and parents. This time she would leave behind part of her heart.

Before Camilla had formulated a farewell speech, Eric pulled her to her feet. "Come with me, if you're warmer. I can't wait to show you this."

Holding her hand, he led her up the stairs to the loft. Camilla wondered on her earlier visits to Eric's house what this room looked like. She had even pictured it in her mind. She had imagined him sweeping her into his arms, carrying her up the stairs, and swearing his undying love for her. Like in the movies. But he hadn't. She blushed, thinking of experiences she and Eric might have shared.

Oh, well. Tomorrow she would be on her way back to New York.

Eric led her to the room. They faced a wall of windows. To the left under the roof's pitch were seven easels. Each one held a canvas of her secret place, painted from different angles, captured in different lights. Putting his arm about her shoulders, Eric led her from one to the other, pausing to let her take each one in.

"I thought this spot was the most peaceful, beautiful place I'd ever seen. It was one of the reasons I bought this house and land. I tried over and over to put on canvas the way that being there by the streams made me feel. But there always seemed to be something missing, something haunting about the place that I could never quite capture. That emptiness made the place even more special to me." Eric paused, thinking. "I've always felt like I had an emptiness inside me. This place spoke to that part of me."

Across the room on the right side set a larger canvas. Over the easel, a gallery light cast a triangular glow on the painting. The last of the fading sunlight washed in from the windows over the painting, too. The canvas looked like it floated, caught in midair between rays of light.

Camilla drank in the picture. It was the canvas from the day she interrupted him in the woods on her first day home. White mist swirled in the painting's center, surrounding a Camilla who twirled on the moss between the two streams. Eric had transformed her from a jean-clad woman into a nymph-like inhabitant of the quiet glade. Camilla gasped at the delicate beauty of Eric's painting.

"That day you came dancing down the ridge to the streams, curls flying around your face, I knew what I had been unable to put into my paintings. The hollow had been missing something all along. You."

Taking her hands and putting them on his chest, Eric continued, "I think I sensed your energy lingering there even before the day I saw you. When you actually stood there, the hollow became complete."

Pausing, he looked down at her smooth fingers nestling in his rough ones. "The days we've spent together have made me realize you could fill the emptiness inside me, too. I have been content to live simply. But after spending time with you, I wonder if I can be content with simple from now on."

Camilla stared at the painting. She willed tears to stay behind her eyes. Why did he have to say this now? Days ago his words would have thrilled her. She came home to rest and to regroup. Eric had done nothing to make her believe anything more than friendship existed between them. Or that there would be more. She had chosen to go back to New York.

Putting his hand under her chin, Eric turned her face up to his. Searching her eyes, he pleaded, "I know you're leaving for New York tomorrow. Don't say goodbye to me now, Camilla. Don't leave me empty again."

"What about my job? What about my life in New York?" Camilla murmured. "Isn't my life important, too?"

He smiled before he pulled her close. "Sure it is. So important that I'm willing to brave moving to New York, if you tell me you want me to." After a pause Eric added, "As long as occasionally we can come back here to rest. I'm selfish enough to want you just to myself sometimes."

"You'd be willing to come to New York? For me?"

"Yes," he answered against her hair. "For us."

Camilla's mind raced. Career, New York, paintings, vows to never fall in love. At the moment, the most important thoughts were those about this man and the safe feeling of his arms enclosing her. For the first time in her life, Camilla decided to risk vulnerability. To step out from behind the wall of her safe place.

"I do have feelings for you, Eric. More than I realized."

Eric lowered his head so his lips tenderly touched hers. Camilla intended this trip to be one of revitalizing and refocusing, a trip to visit her parents and her special place. She never expected to find this man or the comfort here in his arms.

Eric's kisses grew more insistent, pulling Camilla completely away from thoughts of Lucy's surprise when she met Eric for the first time, thoughts of Eric's paintings being on display in New York, even thoughts of Camilla's own emerging emotions. There would be time later for thinking about those things. Time later for thoughts of forever after. Everything was perfect right here and now. Here in this place.